Occupations

Copyright © Anna Mantzaris 2024

ISBN 978-0-913123-44-7

First published by Galileo Books in 2024

FREEGALILEO.COM

Book design by Adam Robinson

OCCUPATIONS

ANNA MANTZARIS

GALILEO PRESS

For Pauline and Christina

CONTENTS

THE ACCOUNTANT

I ate a piano. *I did!* But only half. More like a quarter.
And no butter.

It was my birthday.

I sauté my food in orange juice. I eat zoodles cooked in
one spritz of coconut oil. I count out ten almonds and
then put half back. And then half again.

I spreadsheet meals and lunchtime workouts and
laminate them in Swarovski crystal sheets. I go on
cleanses so fast I am miles down the road.

I keep track and calculate everyone's lunches. I survey
the Tupperware Graveyard *(RIP, Pasta Primavera!)* on
Friday afternoons. Approaching the caloric discards on

the lunch table before the containers hit the recycling bin.

It's a Who's Who of Who Ate What.

Laura ate almost a whole container of Alfredo Waffles. Again.
I spy remnants of a larger-than-life burger bun! Must have been Bob! Or Mackenzie.
She eats like a big man!
She is a big man!

I go on silent retreats with no food. I sneak sneaky-sneak snacks in through oversized shoes and gaping XXL shirt pockets the size of Plano, Texas.

No one sees. It doesn't count! Eat up!

I plan girl's trips to places like MiraLindaLonda and Valley Gorge, arriving home puffy and regretful.

Steak au poivre. Coconut mousse cake. All those margaritas. Barf.

Back at the office:

The temp ate a Mounds bar.

The boss is off her diet. Again.

That guy in marketing keeps a deep-fryer at his desk!

Good thing I have such a wonderful boyfriend.
Meyers.

Meow. Meow.

But he did eat a hamburger at the game last night.
And his mother brought a dizzy dozen of donuts to
our house. *Meyers eats so much sugar.* Meyers thinks it's
funny I said not to eat ice cream in front of me. Now
he stands behind me.

My co-worker *(Meredith? Marzipan? Macaroon?)* does
not have a boyfriend. She goes on dates and shows up
Monday mornings with written lists of everything the
men did wrong. She writes on Post-its stolen from the
office so she can scribble in the bathroom and shove
them in her pockets.

*She fantasizes about eating a pint of Butterscotch Ripple
naked in bed with my Lemony Dream Meyers!*

Drip, drip, drip, lick, lick, lick.

Now it's Macaroni's birthday. So I start a petition against office birthday cakes. It passes. Or whatever a petition does. No more cakes. *Somehow it happened!* I lobbied like I was on the Hill.

I ignore the glances. Macadamia and the other November Babies who were anticipating their chocolate ganache are seething. But I've done them a favor so big it will fill their greedy, growing stomachs like a big rig of rice cakes.

I should be thanked.

I am the grocery shopper who takes inventory of what's on the conveyor belt ahead of others. Saturday afternoon my glare literally sears a woman's head at the grocery store when she buys a bag of chocolate chips and package of butter. She goes to the Emergency Room before returning home with a bandaged head and baking her cookies.

Will nothing stop her?

I keep tracking. On my phone. My steps. My calories. I convert the data to pie charts and graphs and text them to Manicotti who wants to eat my buttery crunchy always-dripping Meyers for *her* lunch.

I've got more steps than you! I had 30 calories less than you this week!
Win. Win.
For me.

I hate Marshmallow. She is a Monstrosity! With her crinkling wrinkling bags of plumping nuts and thick wedges of chorteled cheeses she eats at her crumb-ridden desk.

Right next to mine.

Every night. In my bed. Next to a delicious and snoring Meyers. I have the same fantasy about Marmalade.

She is getting fatter and fatter, blowing up like a parade balloon. Pop!

I am here. In the office. And there. In your office. I am on the plane. I am sitting next to you at the restaurant

where I order hot lemon water or maybe it's the truffle
mac-and-cheese with a side of mashed potatoes this
time and then go home for a cry to Meyers or no one
or the cat or that God damn neighbor who made the
mistake of bringing over his mother's cherry-cherry
hand pies wrapped in bacon fat. *Again.*

I am talented. I can paint. I work on an easel in my
spare room every weekend, painting a Renaissance-
like feast. It's *The Last Supper* meets *The Triumph of
Bacchus*. People are round and big and fat and there
are turkey legs and goblets and grapes. The people are
rolling on the ground and falling off their chairs. They
are smiling and laughing. I cover up the painting with
a big white sheet at the end of each of my sessions. I
remember to double the sheet, for if you look close
enough, through the thin layer of fabric, you'll see my
face smack in the middle of a gluttonous meal.

THE CLEANING WOMAN

I am used to other people's messes. I find ham
sandwiches and pornography stuck together with
store-bought peanut butter on family china shelved
under beds. I pour days-old milk down the sink
so thick it latches and bubbles at the drain before
speaking to me in an undefinable hiss. I scrape purple-
pink-purple-again bubble gum off velvety velvet sofas
with toothpicks so tiny you can't see.

I have seen a lot of dirt.

I detach. I let go. I forgive my first boyfriend for
thinking we could be grownups in a faltering log
cabin with a straw bed and no roof and all those
repercussions. How else could I scrub the toilets now
with my bare hands in pearls and keep grinning.

My house is big. And empty. Even the dog goes to a
daycare. She swims and runs in a field. Her golden
mane shinier than mine. Her name is Maisy but I call
her Artemis. In my head. And dream of her sturdy legs
roaming for the moon with a bow and arrow on her
furry back.

What is that hissing from the sink? asks my husband.

I find a love note. Not to me. I find a picture. Not of
me. A woman dressed in a torn mermaid costume
who is stunningly beautiful even with three eyes is fly
fishing through the air of *my* home, daring me with
her sly smile. I can hear her voice. It's grainy and soft
and seductive too, as she asks where I keep the wine.
I want to look away. Scrub away. Rinse down the sink
with dishwater so hot it freezes my faltering feet stiff
into the linoleum.

I dream about being the dog.

I throw my husband's laptop in the washing machine
and watch it go around. And around. Disintegrating in
detergent. *All clean, Dear!*

I drip dry the keyboard hanging it pristinely with the clothespins from my once-golden hair. I will greet him and tell him how happy I am to see him. *Because it's true.* More true than when we met. At the Mardi Gras party on a snowy afternoon when he draped me in cheap throws before asking my name.

He announces the planned power outage.

I step out in the evening air. On a neighborhood street I have never seen so dark. And for once. On this blind alley. I am so thankful. No flickering blue televisions in upstairs windows. No unnamable whirling and buzzing. No bees in my bonnet or wasps in my very lacy dress.

The other wives are outside. Bobbing their feathered heads, picking up pieces of driveway gravel with their mouths and spitting them out like a flock.

Circle up, Ladies!

You aren't going out in this?

Fuck you, I say.

Thank you! they hear.

And they wave. And wave. And wave. And wave. Their already bony hands becoming the size of small mittens as I pull away.

I move through the deadest 18-way stop in town. Like a broken-down movie set. While the others wait. Polite and slow.

No, you go.

No, you.

No.

Me?

You.

Me?

You.

THE FLIGHT ATTENDANT

You do not leave the wounded ground. Your feet firmly planted. On the sidewalk. On the playground. Where the other moms stand.

On the backyard grass at the neighborhood picnic. The walls are papered in gingham. You never forget the basket. Full of the best muscadine grapes. The size of cat heads.

Your purse is a hot air balloon of snacks. Swollen with nuts and crackers and little beverages with littler pipette straws for those tiny and sometimes big mouths.

You consider asking for a beverage cart for the holidays! Wouldn't it be great to bring everyone what they wanted all at once?

Everyone in this family flies First Class.

You do not own a suitcase for yourself. But you know how to pack. Better than anyone. *Ever.* Deflating an Alpaca sweater down to the size of an eraser. Floating a hot-ironed shirt, defying it to wrinkle. *I dare you.*

You will bring the supersized suitcases up from the gold-painted basement and down from the Montana closets. You will suction out the air of clothes so tight they become airless carcasses.

They look kind of beautiful, no?

You will roll clothes like Italian donuts in turbinado sugar. You will zip-zip-zip-lock-it-up vitamins and shampoos and special creams you compound yourself. You will pick up prescriptions and schedule departure haircuts and get the dry cleaning so dry with perk and poly it simmers in the sun. *For them. Always.*

You will send forgotten work files by raven and say, *I'm so sorry it wasn't in there.* And mean it.

You will attend to, and cater to, and …

You will send your kids to camp with holograms of Broadway stars and pedigreed zoo animals. You will send your kids to college where they import a Japanese teahouse for campus. You will send your husband on business trips. *Let me just whip up a peach cobbler for you. For the road!*

But he will still roam. Before returning home. To your warm and oh-so-desperate range top.

You will do train and airport drop-offs. Bringing your family right on the tarmac. Carrying them up the runway.

But you will not go to the bus station. No one ever takes the bus. Not even the kids.

Not even the dog.

You will keep up your appearance. *You are the best groomed pup in town!* Nails trimmed. Obedient tail at

the ready. You will look good. You will act nice. You
will smile and say, *Welcome aboard!*

You will take the bus.

After they've all gone and the silence of the house
muffles you like a hot snow. And you'll be Frigidaired
at the graying station as you sit on the splintering and
oh-so-shiny bench. A collapsing vending machine
to feed the non-existent travelers clinks nearby with
fallen nickels.

No one will ever look for you in such a place. Soon
you will take off, seated next to someone who found a
hatchet in the riverbed.

THE DETECTIVE

Forget the sleazy storefront agency. I am here. Next to you. Dressed in a fraying trench coat with sunglasses made from an owl. I am living in celluloid. In a piece of black-and-white 16-millimeter film, cut hard and pasted fast on a sticky floor of a once movie-plex.

This is where everything happens.

Awareness is just a game of chance. An elevator to Louis Malle's gallows—void of the pleasure of Miles Davis this time, the sad commuter brass train in his trumpet.

The discovery of the first inciting evidence is always by accident:

- A shrunken wine receipt found at the Phoenix All-Night Desert Museum
- A charge on a credit card for *The Happiness I Deserve*
- Type XoX Blood that doesn't match mine
- A phone bill with multiple calls to a woman with wings
- A voice so tinny and small
- A hatchet with a surprisingly sharp edge

I will place these items in an Evidence bag. The kind used for severed fingers and straying hairs stuck on shagging carpets with thick and torrid bodily fluids. I will hold each up as proof that I am faltering. Falling. Failing. *You win!*

And, of course. The closing argument. Deftly done in his prussic acid voice:

You're writing fiction again.

That one gets me to the bare side of burning insecticides left as coffee.

I do write fiction.

I have lost my confidence to brush my teeth any
way other than sideways hail and make whispered,
cotton-mouthed calls to no one from the laundry room
piled with tax files and photographs that need to be
scrubbed of their dizzying thumbprints. *Keep going!*

There was once another famous man who came into
my life. Early on. When I dressed in coils. Gold lamé.
Hair up. *Who could blame him?*

The famous man received postcards and tiny chairs
and ostrich feathers as fan mail.

Or were they?

And then he left me to eat lemon drops with Anjelica
Huston. Or at least that's who I thought it was. The
sun was too bright to look. And I was scared I would
burn my eyeballs again.

So here we are now. My lover hides his phone that has
grown so big—it's so full of sweet nothings—it lies,
puffy and swollen like an infected meringue. *What fun
for him!*

More clues:

-       He smells different, of course. Like someone's
        almost-turning zest piled on a scorched cake

*I'm going out to get a tire fixed and it can only be done in a
hot air balloon that takes off at 11pm*

-       He brings home presents. I feel like a prized pony
        brushing myself like a horse!

*I'm getting my hair cut at the only all-night barber three
states away*

-       He looks different. Did he always have three ears?

*I need to capture some stars for work tomorrow and it must
be done in the dead of night*

So I give you that. The backstory as quenching as
a blossomy gin + tonic at midnight. A flashback. A
clue to how I got here *again* so we can all do the math
together. Correctly this time:

I can only afford to work part-time, which is 168 hours
a week x 62 + sleepless nights eight days a week in
morning overdrive.

And overdrive I do. With a satchel packed to states I
don't recognize. With foreign language requirements
I master on the way as night continues to fall down.
Around me. To hide what I've brought to throw out
into the dark.

THE BAKER

I will measure and swiftly sift. I will do so carefully.
While I think of my ricrac past like a hem on a
faltering dress. *That is still too pretty to let go of.*

There is no buttery butter so buttery you could melt.
Or rabbit sugar flour. No spiked vanilla soliciting a
hungry chicken for her precious egg.

But still. I carefully gather desert clay near the saguaro
and tap it into small spheres on my typewriter that
was given to me by a poet—who asked for it back
before I smothered him with trays of marzipan. And
an ill-chosen sonnet, while he begged and tossed his
liquor-laced almond hair that smelled sweeter than
mine. His work piling up in bound books. *Before my
eyes.*

I knead and push. I go from past to future to future again on the page. I go to future too much!

I am so far ahead I am in outer space—all by next week.

I am making something. It's not precious. I carve up my 1,123-layer brick into the shape of a baby elephant. But it is only half-baked. I cut so much his ear collapses. His trunk becomes misshapen. But he is still in there. *Somewhere.*

I take him to the glorious party with *so much champagne.* Where he is promptly ignored by the poet's friends that he warned me about—one who will catch an illegal chartered plane with no wings at midnight, another who grabs my chin with his damp and dripping palm. *Good to meet you!*

In the kitchen, in my makeshift apron comprised of sweet fallen ivy that once gently hung on hungry whales, I fold shiny gold boxes for my friends and fill with good luck charms. *Talismans. Amulets. Madstones.* All with letters I harvest in the field to the sound of a snug snail playing a banjo and singing a sorrowful song.

I can't afford a kiln so I hover my hands above the
keys until the house with butterfly painted walls fills
so full up. So full with what is new and strong and still
teetering inside me.

I am not sure how to leave this kitchen.

So I sit here. Where it's warm. And oh-so-sweet. And
keep telling myself the whole story. Until I understand
why I took your notebook. And worn shoes with
fraying laces. And the lucky penny you said I'd never
forget. And left you in the rain of the monsoon. For
dead.

THE FIREFIGHTER

I do not have protective gear. I'm unarmed. Sometimes even ill-equipped. But I'm always the first to smell the faint smoke as it looms in the domestic air. Sometimes a blaze bursts out without warning. Dressed in my sooty pearls and dampened hair still held together in a thoughtful twist, I will roll up the sleeves of my silk dress.

I'm here.

The husband is in crisis. The child in tears. The teenager has slammed a door or gone to the garage or taken a bicycle out after dusk with no plan to return. There are no hoses or ladders. No loyal Dalmatian. But the Golden Retriever will do.

I know how to cool things down. Smooth things over
as if the daily dilemmas were smoldering campfires.
Cigarettes left carelessly burning. Disasters to be
averted. Sometimes thick white ash falls in the living
room. Landing like white snow. Like the remnants of a
husband's affair that burned down walls, leaving only
an acrid smell.

I keep a shovel on the nightstand.

Sometimes the calls come in from far away. A friend, a
co-worker, a relative who is only in touch in times of
crisis. Scalding heat and flying embers come barreling
through a phone connection desperate for help. *This is
an emergency.*

They don't realize this Firefighter has secrets of her
own. Maps of betrayal. Love letters now used as
kindling scorched beyond recognition. Sometimes I
even set the fires myself.

Don't tell anyone.

When I was young I feared I might spontaneously
combust. Erupt into flames. Fall to ash and disappear
in the Earth. Some nights the sounds of a crackling

campfire, the family happily gathered around, reminds
me of this but I tell no one there was a time when I
almost fell apart, came so close.

No hope of rising like a Phoenix.

I'm caught between time and space. Spilling cool
water on the source. Gossip. Misunderstandings.
Long-held grudges. Lives can be at stake. But most of
the time. Not. Usually the fire is small, unassuming.
Sometimes flamboyant like a Baked Alaska with
charred meringue designed to fool and wow dinner
party guests. It comes out burning bright and soon
irreplaceable. But before it's served. Before the chatter
ends and the wine glasses are rinsed, I will step
outside, through the back sliding door, closing the
sound of the others behind me. I will crane my neck
and look up. And I will remember there was a time
when I used to dream I was phosphorescent, like a
carefree firefly lighting up the nighttime sky.

THE CURATOR

Careful. Calculated. Controlled. I am a planner.
Meticulous about details most would never think
of with a vision for a space before I carefully place
myself like a piece of art—perfectly coiffed, carefully
trimmed. No stray thread. *Every time.*

Sometimes I call myself.
From one phone to another.
To hear what I sound like.

I help my husband tie the perfect Windsor knot, lacing
it so close to his throat apple before insisting he take
it off. *Too formal for a Saturday get together for a game
of Whist.* I take away his bourbon and soda or vodka
on the rocks or kerosene he spikes with lime. I dress
the children in sixteen matching outfits for their brief

appearance *(Smile!)* before they *willingly* go up to bed
with pasted grins on their lost and unknowing faces. *I
do love them so.*

Long before the family is ready, before the guests
arrive for slow-roasted lamb with wild oregano that
I harvest before sunrise in the rolling field, I carefully
acquire, collect and catalogue everything in the space.
*A white sofa with kids? How do you do it? Is that the
pottery from Shellie's co-op?*

*The pair of Swedish clogs that double as stilts bought at the
boutique in Poughkeepsie Heights are perfectly forgotten,
left by the velvet tufted ottoman as if they were just thrown
off to read Sigrid Nunez's latest novel that happens to be on
an end table.*

It's so good!

The yellow dog has been outfitted in an upcycled wool
bandana in a jaunty plaid.

He isn't happy about it.

Here's what you don't know about me. I have eight
legs, that's how I move so fast. I know just how to
stand to create an illusion of simply two.

I survey the space before placing down a charcuterie
board piled high with California figs, ribbons of cured
prosciutto, knobs of soft cheese—so big they are
mistaken for Sunday snowballs—rolled in crushed
green peppercorns. Each imported separately. And
served with a cruelty-free baguette. *Always be kind to
the yeast.*

I scan and check my surroundings as if I am the
newcomer. A visitor. An outsider invited in for a
coveted peek. *So this it was it's like inside.*

I am a museum goer. A gallery visitor. In my own
home. *I sell myself a ticket to the museum of prepared
spontaneity.*

My job begins when the guests arrive. I steer
conversations like a big rig on an icy road. There
are chains on my tires. I carefully maneuver like the
tightrope walker who never falters. As the night goes
on, I pour larger and larger glasses of wine gloriously

enormous, except for my husband who gets a
thimble's worth.

Stage direction for me: Act shocked but still partake
when Susan's husband takes out a joint. *We never get
high! Well, not very often anymore.*

I want you to know I can hear my guests but I don't
understand a thing they are saying.

Now the husband is snoring. I slip out of my dress and
into a rose-print kimono and say, *I'll be right up* to his
increasing laryngeal vibration.

It will take me eight days to rinse the dishes. To redust
the living room. To rearrange everything that was
rearranged just hours prior. But I am good at my jobs. I
excel at everything I do.

Don't I? Yes. Don't I? Yes! Don't I? Yes!
Don't I? Yes. Don't I? Yes! Don't I? Yes!
Don't I? Yes. Don't I? Yes! Don't I? Yes!

I sit on the edge of the ottoman as the suns starts
peeking up, sipping a bit more wine I've poured.
I will commend myself on a job well done. On an

ideal show. *Almost. Not quite. The lamb was a little dry. Were the farro-studded avocado "grenades" offensive? The meringue slightly crooked. Maybe the party should have coincided with the space launch. With a rocket takeoff timed with the flambé!*

I think about the launch set for tomorrow. I imagine a compressed cylinder shooting above the atmosphere. I see the fiery streams of fuel as it takes off. I think of the small beads of condensation that will form on the metal I'd like to dab off. As it lifts above the golden atmosphere.

Where the air is thinner and gravity dissipates. Where an imaginary tap has been left on next to crumbs on a non-existent counter. With Virginia's pages floating above an invisible shelf.

THE LIGHTHOUSE KEEPER

Near and far. Sometimes isolated on a rainy archipelago with cowering ironwood trees. Sometimes smack down in an urban center. Remember seeing the cylinder of a building topped with a cupola tucked behind the old sugar refinery?

You are there now.

The Lighthouse Keeper whispers in an undefinable and circular language during unclockable hours while looking out at the dark, dark sea.

There is a translation: *It was the first snowstorm. The train went by and everyone seemed to have disappeared. He was there. Standing in the white drift, wearing his plaid wool coat, tousled blonde hair, standing in all his beautiful*

tallness. He smelled of cedar and smoke in the very best way.
Waiting. And warm inside to the lip's touch.

The lighthouse is empty now, except for you and the
misplaced Northern mockingbird who comes by and
flutters his soon-to-be iridescent wings. He knows not
to linger.

You won't wind clocks, or trim wicks or signal the
fog. Your tasks are determined by boys lost to their
irresistible and never-ending eddy of ancient mariner
destruction. You keep a light on, hoping. *I didn't cause
it. I can't control it.* Everyone knows the beacon doesn't
always work. Everyone but those who wait and hope
for addiction masked as a carnival of confusion tied in
a spiny twine to *please, please go away.*

A friend. A historian. A person of letters knows
it is mainly women who have long cared for the
lighthouses, after husbands have been drunk by
gulping waves. After boats that never return. After
high seas and unspeakable overboards. The wives
who still cook a cioppino that will boil down before it
can be served.

Insomnia is a gift. You stay up at night, creating, waiting and keeping the light on. A constant lookout. You can't sleep if they are not safe. *And they never are.* They are usually out of range but you will not give up listening. You tuck yourself into a soft beige sweater embroidered with fading butterflies that can't keep you warm. Your steaming mug of blackberry tea goes instantly cold. How can you Let Go? *Detach.* Your instinct is the opposite. Hold on as tight as possible. Hold on as if you were in the rocking and dangerous skiff with its fading and splintered cedar hull. Oars so heavy they make arms ache with an almost feeling of pride.

The network of Lighthouse Keepers reaches across the sky like Andromeda. There are so many to keep a light on for. Navigation will determine a path. Sometimes into the light, but most often into the murky violence and lies. An arc of visibility is a farfetched hope. Stuck in a sandbar. On a reef. Washed up on a rocky coastline.

You know isophase light works to a rhythm with equal periods of light and darkness. That's how it began. *He was funny. He was smart. He used to bring straw flowers with him from the warm part of Antarctica.*

But then the darkness becomes longer, the light
dissipates like winters in Alaska, inevitable and so
predictable. Uninteresting to most. The Lighthouse
Keepers own bodies lose a rhythm without the sun.
You become tired, your own light starting to dim.
"Remember when you were this girl?" a sister says one
day, holding up a photo when you'd been caught by a
Nikon laughing on a terrace in Positano.

A Mariner's Warning System of bells and whistles
will become the norm. There is one thing for certain.
A loud chaos in addiction. The navigation becomes
confused. The money goes missing. The lies mount.
The affairs start. You are dizzy from the spiral
staircases you ascend and descend multiple times a
day. You check. And monitor. And wait. Sometimes
you plead and beg. Sometimes you cry and yell.
But mostly you whisper. *I would like to be safe. In the
Lighthouse. With you.*

THE TAXI DRIVER

You know I can't drive. I was confused by the test.
How could I stay at ground control Major You and
stop on command and bake *torticas* and brush my hair
and wash the dishes—all at the same time. *And go so
long without looking down to wash the fiction off my hands.*

But I do drive now. People and luggage come in
and out. Sometimes they bring Ferris wheels. Or
sunflowers. I help gently fold into the velvet-lined
trunk. I carefully maneuver the boulevards. I close my
eyes most of the time. *I am too scared to look out to the
future.*

So I drive only at night. Inching the car above the
cobblestone lanes and forgetting about the signage
written by children in Castilian.

In Cuba. You were on your own. *So I would be too.* I
walked in the humid river overhead. Until a woman.
In a taxi much like my own. Picked me up. Hoisted me
over her pristine shoulder. Then she filled up the car
with other women. We drove to a hospital to drop two
off. I kept asking if she knew where she was going. We
ate overripe bananas and small dots of fresh bread and
cotton candy spun on the dashboard. We stopped in
front of houses and carnivals and more women got out
and more came in.

I was certain we passed you a few times.

Today I am no longer valid in the State's eyes. Or even
in the hamlet where we always resided. My license
is in a permanent state of suspension. I don't like my
photo. I can't look at it. I asked them to replace it with
a picture of a small gold key. Or a soft piece of felt
taped into the corner, *just so.* It felt like a good idea.
At the time. But instead they removed my address,
blacked it out with a Sharpie marker. It was listed as
where we lived for too long.

I am not even recognized there.

My meter is tic-tick-ticking, like how I feel about
myself, but the numbers go so far down and land on
Pi, which is how my father signs his name. I like it
that way. I don't want to charge. Anyone. Anything.
Forever.

I took the partition down with soft hatchet blows and
some gum because I want to talk. And people do talk
to me. Mostly men. Who want to know how I got here.
At this time. *How strange!* They say. Sometimes they
have wives. One tells me his wife has gotten too old.
One tells me his wife never lets him play music in
the house. Another says he lives with a woman who
doesn't let him dance on the living room ceiling in his
gravity boots at midnight.

I get the unlisted phone numbers of these wives
and through the phone cord send them peonies and
leather-bound books and small bottles of fresh jasmine
to dab on their soft toes and sign the notes.

Forever yours

besos

In Cuba the driver, with her elegant neck, brought me
home as dusk was coming to a close and morning was

coming out of a tropical envelope with tamarind juice
raining down for the children. And I heard her words.
Soft and loud and soft again.

Inside. In the harsh light. Where we slept on a cool, flat
rock. You said you were followed by a pack of wild
dogs and couldn't find your way back to me.

But the truth is. You kissed me like a hundred hungry birds.
Until my eyes bled.

THE ARCHITECT

Alone is different from lonely. It took a while to
realize that. You have come from noise. From constant
companionship. *Not all of it was bad.* There was a dog.
Sometimes a child. And now it's quiet. And there is a
lot to do.

The drafting board may be a lap, a writing desk, a
kitchen table—it grows larger each day. There are no
official blueprints but there are plans to rebuild. *Where
will the walls go?* You need to step back. *Will the arches
carry the weight of the Gothic windows?* See the bigger
picture. *How many staircases does one woman need?*

You must be a visionary. But it can be hard to find
inspiration. Sometimes buildings collapse. You know
this. *How long can you live as walls crumble around you*

*like Havana ruins from a Havisham house with so many
once Great Expectations?*

So now you will get out of bed. Too early most
days. Make piping hot coffee—in the octagonal
macchinetta—and sip. You have a kitchen cabinet with
breadcrumbs and cinnamon. *It's a start!*

People say you are brave but you are so scared.

You are caught in a misinterpretation of your life.
Sometimes you close your eyes in front of unfinished
new plans and for just a moment, allow yourself to go
back inside.

You know you shouldn't. Everyone tells you not to.

You smell the jasmine by the front door, wander into
the living room you once loved gessoed with art.
Recall the sound of *him* asking how your day was.
You smell gravy simmering on the stove. You hear
the patter of the dog running up and down the long
railroad hall. You will not stay long.

That place no longer exists.

You put lead to paper. And work. And erase. And
work more through nightfall—until the child,
Esmeralda, falls asleep and wakens, hungry for you.

THE FORTUNE TELLER

I send postcards into the future. The mail flies by night express without postage. Just a small inky imprint from my palm as a designated stamp. Plus a tiny feather. For lightness.

I write this tomorrow:

I wish it were twenty-one-and-a-half Wednesdays ago.

So you would still be here.

Trying to know me.

While I unravel my silk stockings.

I'm a visionary. Often with a fuzzy outlook. I work out of a rented storefront. No crystal ball. Or beaded doorway. More books than fingers. No cash on the premises. What I care about is hidden in folds of time. In words spoken in coriander. And gentle gesture.

Know Tomorrow Today

That's what it says on the invisible fluorescent sign out front.

I tap into small things.

Today's coffee will be bitter but adored. Tomorrow's will not. A cat that needs a home will find it only to leave again at daybreak. An overdue book of world maps won't be returned by infinity. Portugal will be flooded in wine. That I took from the newspaper.

This information is not useful. But I see it. Floating around me. And I offer it up to unaware visitors who wander in off the street before a matinee or on their way to a party where a woman who wears a polka dotted gold shawl with threads unraveling will host, wishing she wore a silk dress embroidered with small birds.

My ancestors read sunflowers. Now, I spread out my own Tarot cards. The Moon. The Lovers. A Wheel of Fortune. A Seven of Cups for daydreaming.

I pull out the Star card. A woman with hair hanging down her back. Kneeling over water. Illuminated by sky. Blessed by chance. And like me. With magnificent new oars. And a compass. Made from all the never-ending hours.

The future can't be seen with the past hovering.

An empath. A clairvoyant. A space wife. Call me what you like. No one's vision of the future is clear. But I try and offer. And help. And mend. And look closer and tighter. To see and witness my own future. Once again. Uncertain but hopeful. A small flickering lantern. At the edge of the world.

THE POET (THE LOVER)

I need structure. I need a swimming pool of parameter
with ebbing, wavy line boundaries. Even if I didn't
know what those were. Until yesterday. And
sometimes. I am still hovering. And unsure.

I am a lover. Out. In the world. Now. On my own.
Which for some reason reminds me of the Number
5. Large and in a cobalt blue. Only one other person
would think this. And we have met. Just once.
Through a landline in non-existence.

*But I remember. How you spoke. To me. Like your beloved
cashmere lop.*

On a Friday afternoon I take a walk. Through sixteen
neighborhoods. It takes several days but it's still

Friday afternoon. I pass the museum where my once-
husband is on display. Encased in beveled glass with a
list of who he was. I go through the words and phrases
in my head. On my arm. In my purse. And then I look
for more. On the ground. Found. *Does not want. The
answer which was. Who knows!*

I hold the new syllables close to me, in a patinaed box.
I am careful not to let them spill and fray and puddle.

I am thinking about practical things. Coffee. A light
bill. An unresponded call. I grasp on to these things.
These essentials.

I have not forgotten the space between stanzas. The
open lines. The missing punctuation. It's a respite.
A way home. A space on a page I secretly saved for
myself.

That one thing.

It's so late it's early morning for bed. A caracara
comes, confused. And off-kilter. But it's OK. He has
dew berries in his mouth. Or grapes. And he may
really be a kind, small dog with a ringed tail. Who is
carrying a petite bottle of champagne.

All good kittens must come to an end.

You used to say that to me before slipping away.

Today at the strike of noon I will sink into the cool sunflower sheets. I will stretch out. I will fill the empty space in the yellow room with the found words:

My

Little

Minty

Very

Minky

I string them together. Like a carnival banner. Or a prayer flag. I pin it up when I am ready. To be tasted. And playfully tousled. Once again.

THE FUNERAL DIRECTOR

Bright orange. Shades of chartreuse and sunflower blue. *Grief is not in charge.*

I listen to the sepia-infused Polaroid of memories that will no longer be shared because one of us has left. In a hazy maze. So cruel and dark it created its own tunnels below a once-milkshake blue house that dried and crumbled and became too deep to come out of. Even for that nimble little lizard.

There is a mother whose child lived six days. The baby was anticipated. Celebrated. Buried in the small cemetery in the city with the magnificent avocado tree in the center. Marked with a small stone lamb that shows moss can grow anywhere. Even on dew-damp stone. Fitted with ladybugs. Who bless it at night.

No one is a cheerleader of loss. Standing on the
sidelines. Encouraging tears.

*A day becomes a night a night becomes a night that is
a morning and then another. Look out for a spry sun
centering around the corner. There is much that doesn't
happen or need to happen.*

I've seen those in mourning, with good intention take
a walk. Around the block. But end up on that grid.
Without fail. And I will patiently wait. With arms
extended. Until they make it back. Sometimes days.
Or weeks later. They don't know yet that the hallway
is secretly growing a walkway of sturdy and beautiful
straw flowers wrapped in ivy. So I will bark like a
prophet. Reminding them of what's here.

And this is my new secret. Of now. I can align the
moon and stars on never-ending summer days. I let
the dogs run free at night, returning home at dawn
tired and happy and well fed. I believe in the twin
sister in the hot air balloon in the painting at the
museum. Even though we've never met.

But I have my losses. Happened. Just by chance. I
usually keep these to myself. I don't feel sorry for

myself. *Not always. Not very much. Sometimes. Maybe
today.*

I will give away my hand-blocked Japanese fairy tales.
And now. When I make tea in a kettle it dissipates
into the air. The stone cups fade away. The silver floats
from the counter. And in this warm kitchen, I know
my morning of mourning is temporary. A fleeting
thought I won't extend. I let the starry shapes move
around without suffering. Without trying to capture
them. In a torn fishing net where they would escape.

When I write goodbye notes to the departed. Which
I do often. The letters float off the page. In a beautiful
swirl to form their own messages. Often too bright to
read.

Dear Dad. I love you more than ...

Today I sit back. Put down my spoon I am writing
with. The letters take shape. Go somewhere. Become
undead.

THE ELECTRICIAN

You have volts of electricity simmering. You don't create power, but you know how to curve into it, how to make it move through a frisson of circuit breakers.

One day you awoke to your new profession. Giddiness coupled with fear. Nervous with frenetic and unknowing energy. *What's happening to me?*

There will be a man, the first, who makes sculptures out of tar. Displayed in a gallery on the West Side. You'll walk the maze of black oozing art and follow him back home.

You smell like a newly paved road.

The scent is intoxicating and nauseating at the same
time but you'll be enveloped in a bed in a small room
atop a falafel restaurant. You'll be back for more. *Thank
you for taking the subway all the way up here,* he tells you.
And you do. Again and again. Even in the pouring
summer rain. Wearing your leather sandals. And a
fading sundress.

You'll wrap your smooth arms so far around your
forever-never-lover they reach the Aksaja River,
named after a bolt of lightning, where you'll let
the cool water and silt run over your greedy hands
before exploring a body once unknown and almost
dangerous to you.

You'll roam the neighborhood where streets are named
after planets—Saturn, Pluto and Mars—with a man
you meet on a train who holds your body that was
damp from the rain, never asking your name. You will
return to a sublet apartment with a bed that sinks to
the floor in the very best way. *I once lived with a man
and a dog,* you tell him. This is your new universe
where light years still travel 6 trillion miles and a short
eight minutes from the electric sun. *But everything has
changed.* Andromeda may be the closest neighboring

galaxy but you would never know looking up at the foggy nighttime sky.

You'll look back at your profession like a time capsule. The early men. And you'll think about the Ancient Greeks and their two concepts of time—*Chronos,* chronological, sequential, and *Kairos,* where you could slip into an envelope of deep time, a space that couldn't be measured in a calendar or on a map. And sitting in the warmest warm of bath water you'll think about the man who handed you a note you still read. Every third day.

You seem shy but it seems like you have a lot you want to say.

You'll think about how at University you marched with women holding candles as they carried a mattress down Broadway in protest. You'll think about the times you've been lucky to make it back home without knowing it. Power and electricity sometimes go dark without warning. This is something we collectively must learn.

Now, at night, you dream. Currents. Conduits. Fuses and Kilowatts. A nighttime language that translates

into a polarity where you've learned to balance
the light and the dark that fuels an immense and
magnificent power.

THE TOLLBOOTH COLLECTOR

I live in the in-between.

I once whirled by, on my own journey. I handed over a small fee for access to a moment of my life that I couldn't retain. No matter how hard I grappled.

But now I move. Not bills. Not coins. Now I collect memories. Photographs. Scraps of paper. Lists of old lovers that are handed over by anonymous arms. I never see the faces but I take the offerings from soft hands and place them in a large wooden box that I carefully sort through at dusk on Sundays. The ones from Canada, I send back to Canada.

I adorn my glorious booth with photos of friends and family. Those I do not see enough. But are still here. I

keep a dog with me. She once was a Golden Retriever.
But now she's a wonderful white terrier that smells of
freshly spun cotton candy.

I live on a highway with no car of my own. It has long
been abandoned. On a road. In a dark neighborhood
near a cement factory. The key hidden in walls from
my past life. Cassette tapes left behind. Poems that
were once secretly stored in the glove compartment
were mailed away with ribbons as postage. Before it
was too late.

On a 97-degree day when it is supposed to be a
snowing, I will take out a scrap of paper. I am wearing
a dress, the only thing I've saved from my former life.
It's made of blue silk with silver threads sewn into
small rabbits and hemmed so long it brushes against
my ankles when I walk. I write down what no one
needs to know.

It's easy to keep secrets when you have no drivers to
talk to.

At first I thought this occupation was purgatory. My
neck ached and stung from looking back. But I just
had to turn around to breathe in the outdoor air. For
the first time. I eat myself silly on buttered carrots with
fresh herbs from my garden perched on the pitched
rooftop. I've taken down the barrier and people know
to stop anyway. They come with handmade teapots
and first-edition books signed by authors who will
later sit for dinner. When someone says, *how much?* I
tell them I charge by the axle.

I arrange towers of beautifully wrapped presents with
gold bows for anyone who comes by. And before the
sun comes and the deer come and the small dog finds
me, asking to be fed. I will think of this in-between
as a fairy tale. The loudness of my scorched past.
Speeding down the road.

I live near an art center. Large sculptures looming from
the road. At night I'm certain they move, like metal
dinosaurs.

I live in California. There are sea otters who float
on their backs. An unusual place but the crossing is
needed.

I live on a Parisian boulevard with cravats and
parfaited coffees.

I live in Budapest on the side of a pastry shop that
gives away honey cakes and sweet dough filled with
plum jam.

Sometimes a passerby walks by me, as if on a stroll.
Usually it is an old man. Sometimes a young woman.
They are deep in thought and always carry an
umbrella made of typed and printed words. Their
ideas hover in the humid air above them. I step out for
a minute. To acknowledge. To say hello. Even though
I won't get a response. It's okay. It's not needed. I turn
my head up to the luminous night sky. Watch the ideas
go by. And say, *thank you so very much.*

THE LIBRARIAN

I catalogue. And sort. And index. I find myself in orchestrated seas of reference volumes that I'm afraid to admit sometimes have no meaning. Or worse. A lack of order.

My first name is Chaos. Really. My parents meant to name me Chloe but there was confusion. But it suits me and I reorganize disordered and dysregulated call numbers. Botanicals should be interspersed with novels. Why hasn't anyone ever pulled *Reality is Not What it Seems* from quantum theory out of the stacks and put it on a small glass shelf that serendipitously hovers above the others? On every eighth Tuesday of the month I add *The Encyclopedia of Fictional Birds* for twenty-one minutes.

I revisit my personal special collection almost daily. An
inscribed edition of Frank O'Hara's *Lunch Poems* given
to me from a poet on Kaffeklubben Island who lived
on marzipan with his Southern accent so long ago it's
impossible to count the minutes anymore but still I try.
This was before my fading husbands. But I remember.

I keep it next to Grumbach's *50 days of Solitude*
unofficially checked out with expired passport stamps.
I came back to get it when the library was closed,
through a secret crawlspace webbed with night
blooming jasmine.

Remembering is a way of forgetting my teacher told me.
And I do remember. Everything. All the time. A note,
decades old: *It seems you want to be known*. I waited
so long to answer the number at the bottom it was
connected to an extinguished cell tower.

The number you have reached is no longer in existence.

I am cataloguing ephemera. I pull photos and
bookmarks and drawings and tickets and even coins
tucked into cracking spines left behind by unknown
patrons and put them out on a dying world map
to make sense. There are faded twill ribbons in

Wedgewood blue that have become rivers. A silver elephant pendant serves as a city center. A snowy white feather from a mute swan is an out-of-reach mountain range.

I used to be the quietest of all the librarians, the one who didn't dare to speak, even to myself, while amass in citations. Now I have found a hybrid of some unknown format adapted from years of not being able to say what I want. What I need. The citations are in a font so small even I can't see to read them aloud but I know, in there, if anyone looks close enough, they will see the numbers, the alphabets of geography spelled out, showing where my life has gone.

ACKNOWLEDGMENTS

A version of "The Flight Attendant" appeared in *Spry*

A version of "The Accountant" appeared in *New Plains Review*

"The Baker" appeared in *Bending Genres*

"The Detective" appeared in *New World Writing Quarterly*

ANNA MANTZARIS

Anna Mantzaris is a San Francisco-based writer. Her work has appeared in *Ambit, The Cortland Review, McSweeney's Internet Tendency, Necessary Fiction, New World Writing Quarterly, Sonora Review,* and elsewhere. She teaches writing in the M.F.A. program at Bay Path University.

www.ingramcontent.com/pod-product-compliance
Lightning Source LLC
Chambersburg PA
CBHW030418120726
47904CB00007B/2332